Giant Hiccups

Jacqui Farley

illustrated by Pamela Venus

To Dane and Kara Louise

Tamarind Books

© Tamarind 1994   ISBN 1–870516–27–3   Printed in Singapore

Text ©1994 Jacqui Farley   Illustrations ©1994 Pamela Venus   Edited by Anna McQuinn

This impression 1995

Once, at the top of a huge hill
stood a small town
where many people lived and worked.

At the bottom of the hill
loomed an enormous dwelling
where a giant lived.

The giant was called Ayesha.
She never bothered the townspeople
but spent her days quietly.

She made cups and plates
and pots and pans.

She made rainbow lollipops
and pineapple jam.

Suddenly, one day
the ground shook
and a dreadful noise
filled the air.

It sounded
like a hundred dinosaurs
falling out of bed.

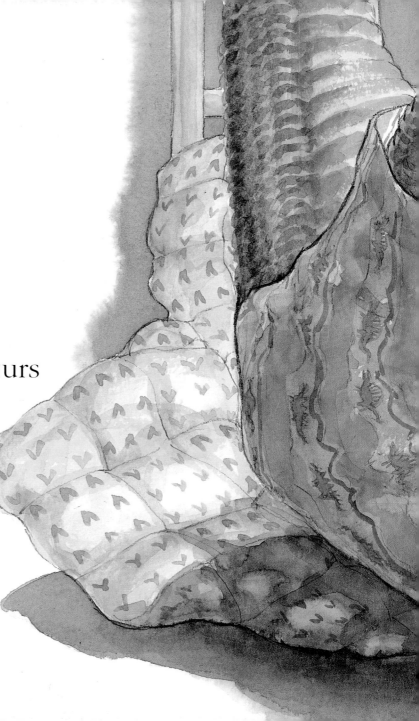

HICCUP!

The small town on the hill trembled.
It shuddered and shook.

In the houses, everything rattled.

One young man wobbled crazily
along the road on his bicycle.

HICCUP!

The children in school
held onto their tables
to stop them falling over.

Books flew.

HICCUP!

The statue of the mayor
fell off its pedestal.
People hurried from everywhere
and met in the square.

"What can it be?" they called.

"What's happening?" they cried.

"It's an earthquake!" said some.

"We have to get off the hill,"
  said the parents taking charge.

They all joined hands
and began to walk down the hill.

HICCUP!

They all slid, head over heels,
right down to the bottom of the hill.

"Wheeee!" shouted the children.
"It's a slide."

Suddenly,
there was another ground-shaking

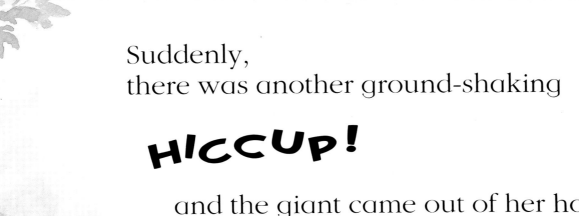

HICCUP!

and the giant came out of her house.
"Hey, you up there," the mail carrier cried,
"you're creating a terrible disturbance.
Stop it at once."

"Our homes are on the hill!"
shouted one of the townspeople.
"Your hiccupping
is destroying our town!"

HICCUP!

said the giant apologetically.

"Perhaps we should give her a drink of water," suggested one old lady.

GLUG, GLUG, GLUG. Ayesha drank it all up.

HICCUP!

"Let's give her a fright,"
the baker whispered to the mail carrier.
The mail carrier whispered
to the lady next to him.
The children whispered to each other.
They passed it on
until everyone knew what to do.

BOOOOOO OO
they all shouted in their loudest voices.

HICCUP!

said the giant.

Miss Wiggins the school teacher,
made a suggestion.
"Try holding your breath for as long as you can,"
she called up to the giant.

Ayesha held her breath,
and held it,
and held it,
and held it for so long,
she had to breathe out with a gigantic
WHOOOOOSHHHHHH!

"I wish I'd brought my kite," laughed Tunde.

But …

HICCUP!

said the giant sadly.

No-one knew what to do next.

Then some children from Miss Wiggins' class put up their hands.
"Maybe she's hungry," said Kara Louise.
"I sometimes get hiccups when I'm hungry," agreed Ben.

HICCUP!

said the giant.

"We might as well try your idea," said Miss Wiggins.

All the townspeople
scrambled off in different directions.

Some collected wood from the forest
to make a huge fire. Others went to the fields
and collected vegetables.

The fire brigade poured water into Ayesha's pot.
Ayesha put in her favourite spices,
and tried very hard not to hiccup too loudly.

"DELICIOUS!" she said. "THANK YOU."

Then everyone noticed something.
The hiccupping had stopped.

Suddenly, there was a tiny HICCUP!

"Oh, Ben! Are you ready for lunch?" said Ayesha.
"Making giant vegetable stew is a hungry business!
I'm sure there's enough to share."

And there was.